Little, Brown and Company

Hachette Book Group
1290 Avenue of the Americas, New York, NY 10104
Visit us at lb-kids.com

Little, Brown and Company is a division of Hachette Book Group, Inc.
The Little, Brown name and logo are trademarks of Hachette Book Group, Inc.

The publisher is not responsible for websites (or their content) that are not owned by the publisher.

First Edition: October 2014

Library of Congress Cataloging-in-Publication Data

London, Olivia.
Welcome to the Everfree Forest! / by Olivia London. — First edition.
pages cm. — (My little pony)
ISBN 978-0-316-28229-1 (pbk) — ISBN 978-0-316-28228-4 (ebook)
I. Title.
PZ7.L8434Wen 2014
[E]—dc23

2014001583

10 9 8 7 6 5 4 3

CW

Printed in the United States of America

Welcome TO THE EVERFREE FOREST!

By Olivia London

LITTLE, BROWN AND COMPANY
New York Boston

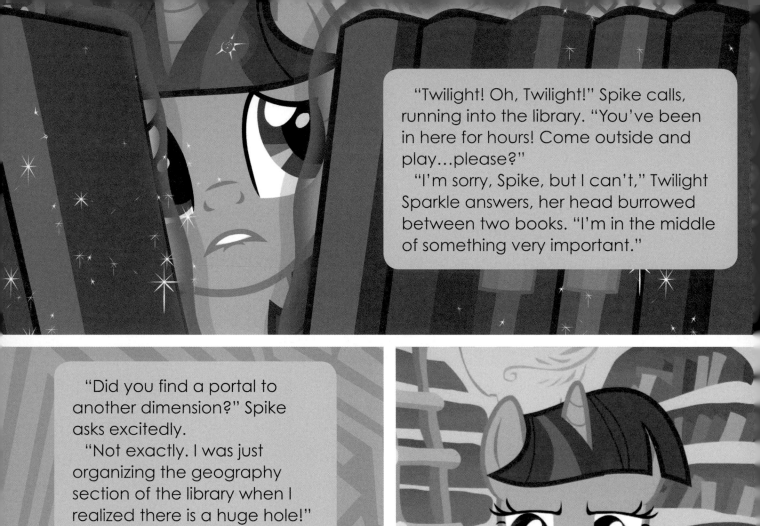

"Twilight! Oh, Twilight!" Spike calls, running into the library. "You've been in here for hours! Come outside and play…please?"

"I'm sorry, Spike, but I can't," Twilight Sparkle answers, her head burrowed between two books. "I'm in the middle of something very important."

"Did you find a portal to another dimension?" Spike asks excitedly.

"Not exactly. I was just organizing the geography section of the library when I realized there is a huge hole!"

"Where? Let me see!" Spike cries out, jumping up. "Maybe it *is* a portal!"

"It's not that kind of hole, Spike," Twilight says.

"Oh. How many different kinds of holes are there?"

"I mean there's a gap in the *information*," Twilight explains. "I have absolutely nothing about the Everfree Forest in here."

"Good," Spike replies. "The Everfree Forest is spooky, and no one should ever go there."

"Without going into the Everfree Forest, I never would have found the Elements of Harmony and been able to save Equestria from Nightmare Moon," Twilight reminds him.

"I guess that's true," Spike agrees.

"I learned a lot about the Everfree Forest from that experience," she says. "In fact, we all did...."

"I know that look, Twilight," Spike says. "You've got an idea!"

"I sure do, Spike," Twilight replies. "Come on! Let's go!"

Twilight and Spike gather their friends together.

"What do you want to talk to us about, Twilight?" Applejack asks.

"I was organizing my library today and realized there's one subject missing from my Equestria section. I need your help to write a book about it."

"Oh my," says Rarity. "I've always wanted to write a book!"

"Is it about the history of the Wonderbolts?" shouts Rainbow Dash.

"Sorry, Rainbow Dash," Twilight says, shaking her head.

"So what *is* it about?" Pinkie Pie asks.

"The Everfree Forest."

There is a rush of murmurs and gasps.

"That Forest is just so dreadful!" Rarity cries.

"But we've all been inside it! We know it best. Sure, it's a little scary, but it should still be remembered as an important part of Equestria," Twilight explains.

"Come on, y'all," Applejack says. "Twilight needs our help!"

The ponies each write a section of the book.

An Introduction to the Everfree Forest

By Twilight Sparkle

When I first moved to Ponyville, I came to oversee the Summer Sun Celebration. I had read about the prophecy of Nightmare Moon and how she would bring nighttime to all of Equestria—forever! The only thing that could save Equestria was reuniting what were known as the Elements of Harmony: Kindness, Laughter, Generosity, Honesty, Loyalty, and one mystery Element.

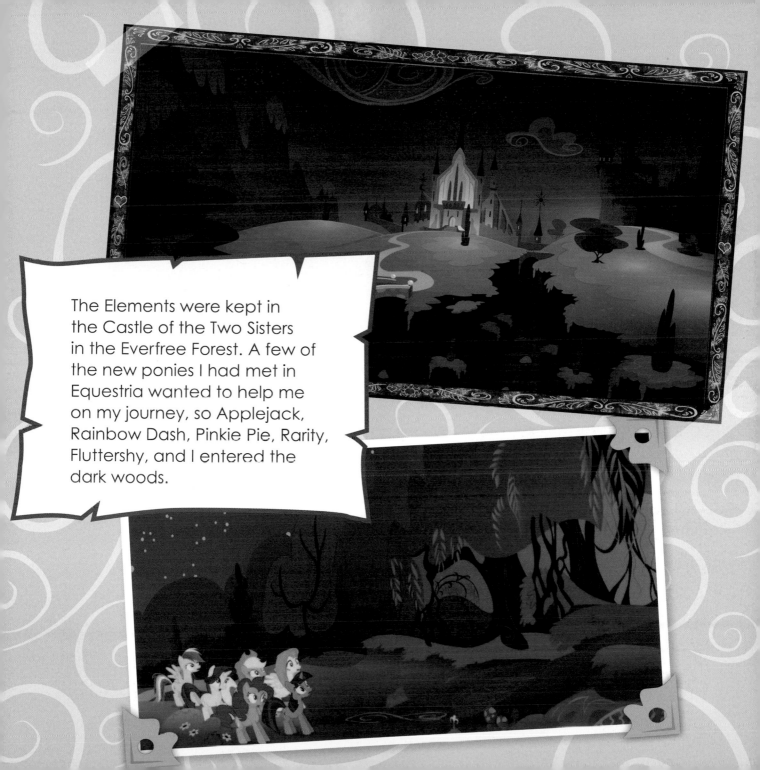

The Elements were kept in the Castle of the Two Sisters in the Everfree Forest. A few of the new ponies I had met in Equestria wanted to help me on my journey, so Applejack, Rainbow Dash, Pinkie Pie, Rarity, Fluttershy, and I entered the dark woods.

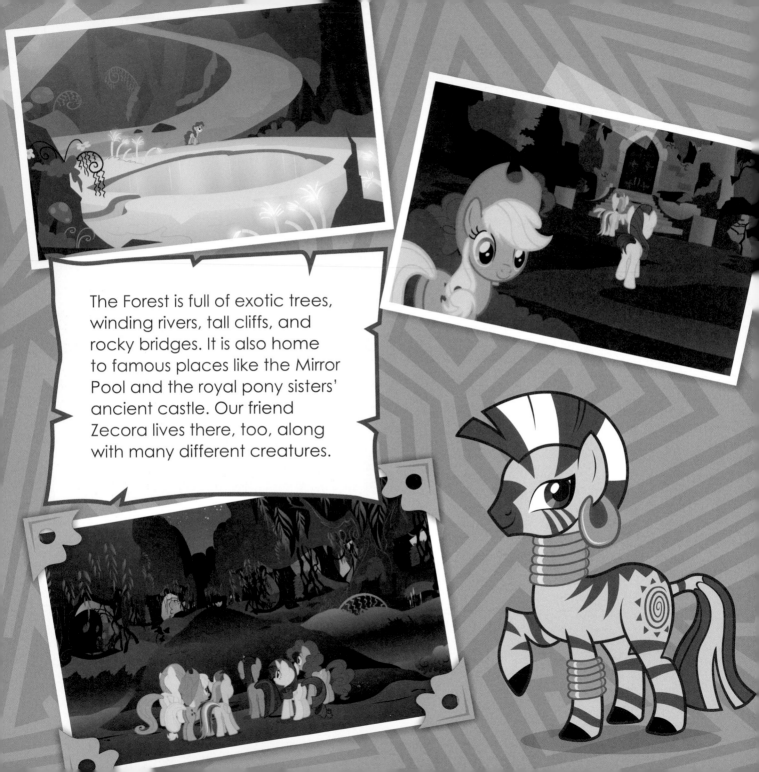

The Forest is full of exotic trees, winding rivers, tall cliffs, and rocky bridges. It is also home to famous places like the Mirror Pool and the royal pony sisters' ancient castle. Our friend Zecora lives there, too, along with many different creatures.

The Castle of the Two Sisters, now in ruins, was home to Princess Celestia and Princess Luna when they were young. The castle held the Elements of Harmony and helped us discover the sixth Element—Magic. My friends are the only reason I am able to put together this booklet containing all the known information about the Everfree Forest.

The Manticore

Manny Roar, a manticore, is a large creature with the body of a lion, the tail of a scorpion, and the wings of a dragon. He seemed awfully scary when we first met him, but he was just in pain! Poor thing had a splinter in his paw. After I removed it, he was the sweetest thing ever.

Parasprites

These tiny, adorable flying creatures look like bees but are much trickier to handle! They devour crops and multiply rapidly, just by coughing! They almost took over our town, until Pinkie Pie cleverly led them back into the Forest with music. Now we know never to take them out of their habitat—or feed them anything!

Ursas

These magical bears with fur that looks like the night sky live deep in the Forest. Ursa Major is the mother; Ursa Minor is the baby. It appears that when they are left alone, they keep to themselves.

Timberwolves

These are by far the scariest animals in the Forest. They look like wolves, only they are bigger and more terrifying, with bright green eyes and an unstoppable hunger. They have been known to chase ponies when they are looking for their next meal! They have very foul breath, and if they break apart, they seem to come back even larger. Definitely beware of timberwolves!

The Cockatrice

This is a curious creature with the head of a chicken and the body of a snake. It has the mysterious ability to turn ponies and animals to stone. I can reverse its stoning effect with "the stare," my gift, but I can't always control it.

ZECORA AND THE SECRET PLANTS AND MEDICINES OF THE EVERFREE FOREST

BY APPLEJACK

A LONG TIME AGO, EVERYPONY WAS AFRAID OF ZECORA, THE ZEBRA WHO LIVES IN THE FOREST. WELL, EVERYPONY EXCEPT MY LITTLE SISTER, APPLE BLOOM. ONE TIME, APPLE BLOOM WENT TO TALK TO ZECORA AND PROVE EVERYPONY WRONG. WE FOUND HER AT THE EDGE OF THE FOREST NEAR A BLUE PLANT. ZECORA TRIED TO WARN US THAT THE PLANT WASN'T SAFE, BUT WE THOUGHT SHE WAS CURSING US! WE ALL TOUCHED IT AND CAME DOWN WITH MYSTERIOUSLY FUNNY SYMPTOMS. THE BLUE PLANT IS CALLED POISON JOKE, AND WHEN WE FOUND OUT IT WAS THE CAUSE OF OUR SICKNESS, BOY, DID WE FEEL SILLY! THAT'S WHEN WE LEARNED YOU SHOULD NEVER JUDGE A BOOK—OR A ZEBRA— BY ITS COVER.

POISON JOKE: THIS BLUE PLANT HAS A BULB IN THE CENTER AND LARGE BLUE PETALS. IT LOOKS LIKE A FLOWER AND LIKES TO PLAY PRACTICAL JOKES ON EVERYPONY WHO TOUCHES IT. WATCH OUT!

SEEDS OF TRUTH: THE FLOWER FROM THESE SEEDS IS THE ONLY KNOWN CURE FOR CUTIE POX, BUT IT WILL ONLY SPROUT FROM HEARING THE TRUTH. THEN, THE PETALS CAN BE EATEN.

The Dark That Lurks Inside the Everfree Forest
By Rarity

We're supposed to be finding nice things to say about the Everfree Forest, but I've found the place to be nothing but dreadful. It's dark and murky, and they say that everything in the Forest works on its own—without any help or forces from inside Equestria. Can you imagine!? The plants grow on their own, the animals take care of themselves, and even the weather changes without help from the ponies. It's just terrifying. I do my best to avoid it whenever possible—and you should, too!

I did meet that lovely sea serpent, Steven Magnet, in the Forest. He was swimming in the river, howling about his mustache. Someone had rudely cut half of it off, poor thing! Still, the Everfree Forest gives me the chills, and that's all I have to say. Now I have a very important dress to design. Ta-ta!

The Mirror Pool

By Pinkie Pie

The Everfree Forest isn't scary at all! It's just smoke and mirrors—all you have to do is laugh. Speaking of mirrors...this one you might want to stay away from. It all started because I was worried that I was missing out on fun with my friends. I wanted to be with everypony at once—and that got me thinking about the legend of the Mirror Pool. So I went into the Forest to find it and wound up cloning way too many Pinkie Pies!

Deep inside the Forest is a pool of magical water. When you recite a specific rhyme, a hole in the ground opens up and you fall through it. When you recite another rhyme, it activates the pool, which turns your reflection into a clone! It can be very dangerous, though, so we closed up the entrance to the pool for good. Still, the Everfree Forest is full of all kinds of cool things like the Mirror Pool. You should totally go inside and explore it!

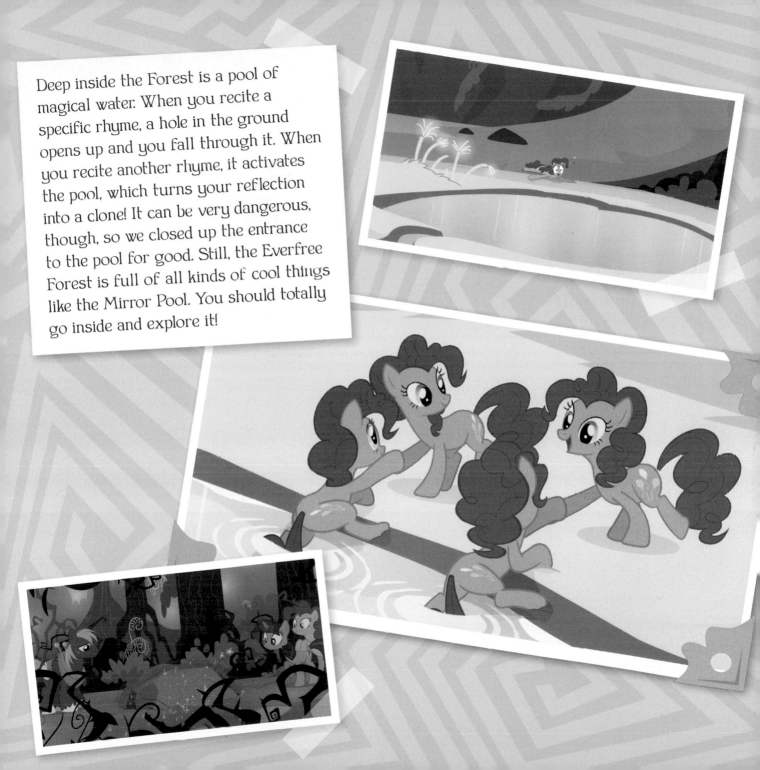

Go On an Adventure!
By Rainbow Dash
This concludes our book on the Everfree Forest. You know everything that we know. You want a little danger in your life? You want to get the adrenaline pumping? Be brave. Take a walk through the Forest!